Paddington Bear
and the Busy Bee Carnival

MICHAEL BOND
Pictures by R. W. ALLEY

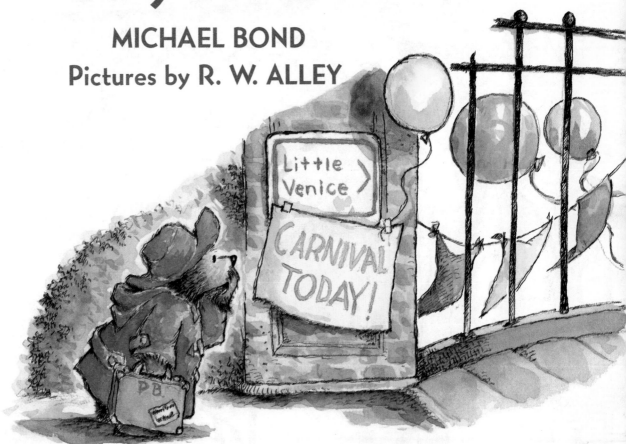

Little Venice >

CARNIVAL TODAY!

PB

2001 Edition
Printed in the USA

📚 HarperCollins*Publishers*

Paddington Bear and the Busy Bee Carnival
Text copyright © 1998 by Michael Bond. Illustrations copyright © 1998 by HarperCollins Publishers.
Printed in the U.S.A. All rights reserved.
Library of Congress catalog card number: 97-71019
❖ http://www.harperchildrens.com

ne day Paddington's friend Mr. Gruber took him on a surprise outing to a part of London known as "Little Venice."

"It's called Little Venice because it's by a canal," he explained, "and every Spring they hold a big Carnival. Boats come from all over the country to take part in the celebration."

Paddington always enjoyed his days out with Mr. Gruber. He waved as one of the boats went past. All the people on board waved back at him.

"I've never been for a ride on a canal before," said Paddington.

"Who knows," said Mr. Gruber mysteriously, "perhaps you will before the day is out. But first of all, we must see what else is happening. We don't want to miss anything important."

He pointed to a board showing all the different events, but there were so many Paddington didn't know which to try first. "How about the Busy Bee Adventure Trail?" suggested Mr. Gruber. "You have to find as many things as possible beginning with the letter B."

Paddington thought that sounded like a very good idea, especially when Mr. Gruber told him the first prize was a free boat ride for two.

"Bears are good at trails, Mr. Gruber," he explained.

Looking around he could already see lots of things beginning with the letter B. Apart from B for BOARD, there was a BOY blowing BUBBLES, a man eating a BAGEL and another with a BROOM, a BARBECUE, and a lady selling BANANAS. There were BOATS everywhere and lots of BALLOONS. There was even a man playing the BANJO in a BAND.

After Paddington had finished writing them all down, he and Mr. Gruber set off along the canal.

In no time at all, Paddington had added five other items to his list: first there was B for BRIDGE, and then BLACKBIRD, BUTTERCUP, BLOSSOM, and BUTTERFLY.

They hadn't gone
very far when they saw
a lady feeding some ducks.

She was wearing a

BONNET, a BLOUSE

fastened at the neck with a BROOCH,

and around her wrist she wore a BRACELET.

When she saw Paddington she smiled and said, "Would
you like some?"

"Thank you very much," said Paddington. He wrote down
BAG and BREAD. He then raised
his hat politely and said,
"Busy Bee Adventure Trails
make you hungry."

"This is the sort of day out I like, Mr. Gruber!" Paddington announced, as he took a jar of marmalade from his suitcase and began making a sandwich.

"Ahem, Mr. Brown." Mr. Gruber gave a cough. "I think you were really meant to give the bread to the ducks."

Before Paddington had time to reply there was a loud buzzing noise and something landed on his marmalade.

Paddington gave the object a hard stare before adding BEE to his list.

Next, they came upon a man fishing.

"I think you've struck lucky, Mr. Brown," whispered Mr. Gruber.

He waited patiently while Paddington wrote down BOX, followed by BERET, BEARD, BELT, BUCKLE, BOOTS, BUCKET, and BASKET.

"Would you like to have a try?" asked the man. "You can use some of my worms if you'd like."

Paddington thought that was a very good idea, but first he wrote down B for BAIT.

"If you're going in for the
Busy Bee competition," said the
man, "you should watch out.
There's a boy following you
and I think he's up to no good."

Paddington was about to say "thank you" when he felt a tug
on the fishing line. "I think it might be too
big to go in my jar, whatever
it is!" he exclaimed.
"It feels like a W
for WHALE."

"I'm not sure you'll find any whales this far inland,

Mr. Brown," said Mr. Gruber tactfully.

All the same, to be on the safe side Mr. Gruber tied some

rope around his friend.

"Strike me pink!" said the fisherman. "It's a BICYCLE!"

Paddington was most disappointed.

"Never mind," said Mr. Gruber. "At least it's another word for your list."

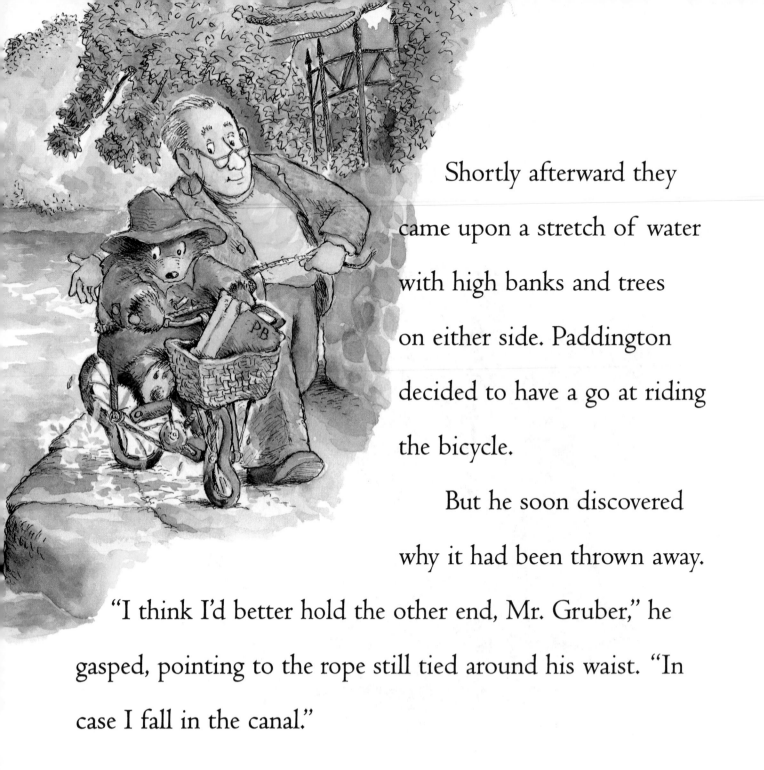

Shortly afterward they came upon a stretch of water with high banks and trees on either side. Paddington decided to have a go at riding the bicycle.

But he soon discovered why it had been thrown away.

"I think I'd better hold the other end, Mr. Gruber," he gasped, pointing to the rope still tied around his waist. "In case I fall in the canal."

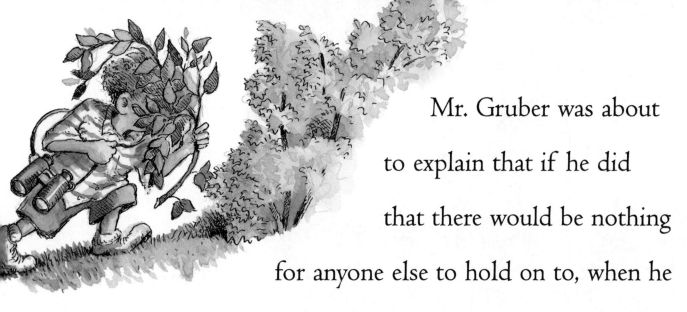

Mr. Gruber was about
to explain that if he did
that there would be nothing
for anyone else to hold on to, when he
saw the look on Paddington's face.

"Is anything the matter, Mr. Brown?" he asked.

"I think we're being followed by
a B for BUSH, Mr. Gruber,"
hissed Paddington.

"Come back!"
shouted Mr. Gruber,
"whoever you are!"
Meanwhile, Paddington
added BINOCULARS to his list.
While he was writing, a boat went past and one of the
passengers had a BABY on her lap. She was feeding him from
a BOTTLE. The baby was wearing a BIB and his sister was
holding a BALL.

Mr. Gruber sat down by the water while Paddington added up his list.

Altogether, with the BANK and BRAMBLES next to Mr. Gruber, he had forty-one things beginning with the letter B.

Mr. Gruber looked at
his watch. "I think it's time we got
back, Mr. Brown," he said. "We don't
want to be late for the judging."

"Good luck," called the fisherman
as they went past.

"We shall be cheering you on," said the lady feeding the ducks.

"Has anyone collected more than forty B's?" called the judge.

"I have!" cried Paddington, waving his piece of paper excitedly. "I've got forty-one."

"So have I!" came a voice from nearby.

Mr. Gruber looked over the boy's shoulder. "This list is exactly the same as young Mr. Brown's," he said sternly. "You must have been copying it— word for word!"

"Oh, dear," said the judge. "We can't have that. I'm afraid I shall have to stop the contest!"

"It's all right, Mr. Gruber!" called Paddington. "We've won. I've thought of another B. That gives me forty-two."

"Fancy nearly forgetting the most important item of all," said Mr. Gruber, as they set off on their boat trip. "What made you think of it?"

"I saw my reflection in the water," explained Paddington.

Mr. Gruber nodded. "It's often the hardest of all to see things that are right under your nose," he said.

"It is if you're a B for BEAR," agreed Paddington. "Bears have very long noses."

It was dark by the time Paddington and Mr. Gruber arrived

back, and the fireworks had already started.

Mr. Gruber bought a packet of sparklers and, as they stood on

the bridge to watch, Paddington joined in with his own display.

With his sparkler he waved

Thank you Mr. Gruber
for a lovely day out!

In the excitement the only person who noticed was

Mr. Gruber himself, but that was really

all that mattered.

"If you ask me, Mr. Brown," said Mr. Gruber, as they made their way home, "the nicest B of all is yet to come."

"I think I know what that is," said Paddington sleepily.

"It's B for BED!"